DANGER! ACTION! TROUBLE! ADVENTURE!

THE D.A.T.A. SET

Invasion of the Insects

By Ada Hopper   Illustrated by Sam Ricks

LITTLE SIMON
New York London Toronto Sydney New Delhi

LITTLE SIMON

An imprint of Simon & Schuster Children's Publishing Division
1230 Avenue of the Americas, New York, New York 10020
First Little Simon hardcover edition April 2017
Copyright © 2017 by Simon & Schuster, Inc.

Designed by John Daly. The text of this book was set in Serifa.
Manufactured in the United States of America 1021 SKY 10 9 8 7 6 5 4 3 2
Library of Congress Cataloging-in-Publication Data
Names: Hopper, Ada, author. | Ricks, Sam, illustrator. Title: Invasion of the insects / by Ada Hopper ; illustrated by Sam Ricks. Description: First Little Simon paperback edition. | New York : Little Simon, 2017. | Series: The DATA Set ; 6 | Summary: "The town of Newtonburg has been invaded by all sorts of creepy-crawlies from mosquitoes to bees to ants and more! What's worse is that they are all mysteriously swarming toward Dr. Bunsen's house when the kids get shrunk down to the size of insects"— Provided by publisher. Identifiers: LCCN 2016029845 | ISBN 9781481471169 (paperback) | ISBN 9781481471176 (hc) | ISBN 9781481471183 (eBook) Subjects: | CYAC: Inventions—Fiction. | Insects—Fiction. | Size—Fiction. | Clubs—Fiction. | Adventure and adventurers—Fiction. | BISAC: JUVENILE FICTION / Readers / Chapter Books. | JUVENILE FICTION / Action & Adventure / General | JUVENILE FICTION / Science Fiction. Classification: LCC PZ7.1.H66 Inv 2017 | DDC [Fic]—dc23
LC record available at https://lccn.loc.gov/2016029845

CONTENTS

Chapter 1	Quit Bugging Me!	7
Chapter 2	Dr. von Naysayer	19
Chapter 3	Bug-Size Zapped	31
Chapter 4	To the Rescue	47
Chapter 5	Don't Look Down!	57
Chapter 6	A Buggy Plan	71
Chapter 7	Beetles and Termites and Bees, Oh My	83
Chapter 8	March of the Ants	93
Chapter 9	Spider Attack!	105
Chapter 10	Dr. B.'s Busy Bees	117

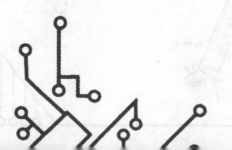

Chapter 1

Quit Bugging Me!

The hot sun shined in through the open tree house window.

"Ugh, guys, I can't take this heat." Cesar sprayed himself with water from a squirt bottle.

"Me either," said Olive, swatting away a mosquito. "Or these bugs."

It was a Saturday morning in

Newtonburg. Gabe, Laura, Cesar, and Olive—otherwise known as the DATA Set—were hanging out in their tree house. Normally the tree house was awesome. But the swarm of bugs flying around made things decidedly *unawesome*.

"Well, it's kind of cool," said Gabe. "I like studying bugs."

"Normally I do too," said Olive. "But I draw the line at stinkbugs. There were seven in my bedroom this morning. And it's true—they really do stink!"

"I woke up with an enormous queen bee in my hair," said Cesar.

"That must have been royally annoying!" Olive joked.

"Hey, good one!" Cesar laughed. "Oh, oh, I got one. Why did the bee keep secrets?"

Olive shrugged. "Why?"

"None of your beeswax!"

Olive and Gabe burst into

laughter as Cesar added, "Or none of your *Bzzzzzzzz-ness!*"

"Hey guys, can you quiet down? I'm almost done repairing the air conditioner," Laura said. She was tinkering with a circuit board.

"Sorry, Laura. I can close the window to keep the bugs out," Olive offered.

"No, don't. This tree house is made of metal," Laura snapped. "The heat will be unbearable if there's no airflow."

"Sorry." Olive plopped down next to Cesar. "I . . . umm, didn't mean to *bug* you."

Cesar chuckled, but Laura didn't think anything was funny.

"If you guys would let me focus,

I could cool down the tree house already," she said.

"Hey, don't blame us. Blame these buzzy bugs!" Cesar shooed a fly away, but the insect chased him around the tree house until he bumped into Laura's table.

SHATTER!

"Oh no! Cesar!" Laura cried. The magnifying lens lay in pieces on the floor.

"Sorry, Laura," Cesar apologized. "I was just trying to escape that fly. Guess *I* turned out to be the buzzkill."

Laura wasn't amused.

"Now I need to go get another lens from Dr. B.," she said with a huff.

"We can go," suggested Gabe.

"No thanks," said Laura as she stepped into the elevator. "You've done enough already. I need some fresh air."

The friends watched Laura ride down and stomp away from the tree house.

Chapter 2

Dr. von Naysayer

"They just don't get it," Laura explained over at Dr. Bunsen's. "They're goofing off while I'm trying to work!"

"Yes, yes." The doctor fiddled with an oversize contraption. Flies buzzed around his head. "Quite a buggy problem!"

"Exactly!" said Laura.

The doctor sighed. "Why, my Bug-Away-400 just won't work!"

"Huh?" Laura asked, confused.

Dr. Bunsen motioned to his invention. "My Bug-Away-400. It's supposed to keep all these insects far away. But alas, there are more bugs in Newtonburg than ever."

Dr. Bunsen pointed to a line of

ants crawling across his desk. "A buggy problem if ever there was one!"

Nearby, a dragonfly flitted in front of a small television playing a news program.

"That's not what I meant—" Laura started, but she was interrupted by the reporter.

"This just in: Dr. von Naysayer has made a giant discovery in the fertilizer industry with his newest brilliant invention!"

A stiff-looking scientist appeared on the screen. "Yes, thank you. I am quite proud," the man said. "My new fertilizer will keep pests away, guaranteed. I make sure my inventions are one hundred percent bug free, unlike some scientists."

"Ugh." Dr. Bunsen groaned. "Speaking of bugs, turn that off."

"Who is that? You know him?" Laura asked.

"He was my old partner, Dr. von Naysayer." Bunsen tossed his tools onto the lab table. "He always thought my ideas were mad. He liked to play it safe and hated taking risks. One day I decided I could not work with such a nay-sayer anymore. I

told him we needed to work together or I would leave. He refused, so I left and haven't spoken to him since." Dr. Bunsen shrugged. "It's okay though. All I need is *science*. And, of course, my lab in this lovely old Victorian house!"

"Right . . . ," said Laura.

"It's also splendid

having four science-loving kids around. You make a great team," Bunsen said with a smile. "But anyway, what was it you wanted?"

"A magnifying lens," Laura said.

"Ah, yes," replied the doctor. "I have just what you need."

Bunsen bounded into a storage room. While he was gone, Laura glanced around the laboratory. Inventions whirred and clicked. The large swarm of bugs approaching the bug-deterrent machine was growing larger. The buzz was unsettling.

Laura suddenly felt bad about snapping at her friends.

"Dr. B.," she called. "I'll come back later. I'm going back to the tree house to talk to the others."

BUG-AWAY-400

The doctor didn't reply.

"Dr. B.?" she repeated. There was a ton of noise coming from the storage room. Laura moved forward to get a better look, but as she walked away from the desk, she bumped into an odd contraption that looked like a reverse microscope.

"Hmm, what does this thing do?" Laura wondered aloud.

The machine began to glow blue, then red, and then . . .

ZAP!

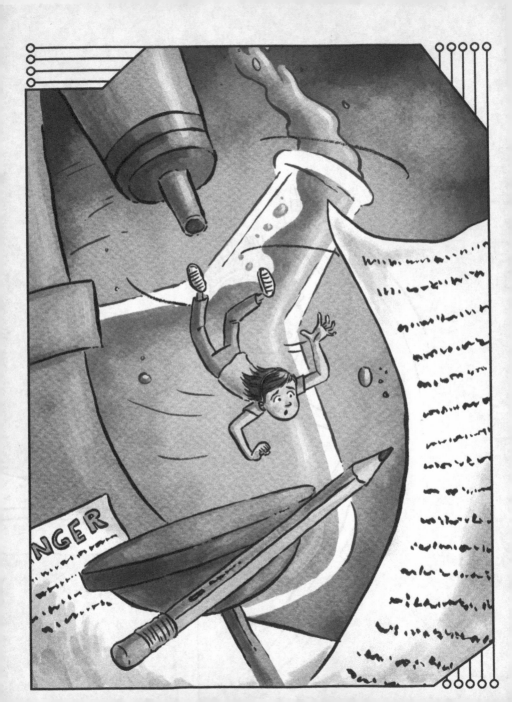

Chapter 3

Bug-Size Zapped

"What's happening!" Laura cried as the room whirled around her. Everything in the lab was growing bigger and bigger!

Plop! She landed on Bunsen's desk. It was the size of a football field. In fact, all the lab equipment had become enormous. She was surrounded by giant microscopes. Giant goggles. Giant flasks. Even a giant flying creature was zooming right toward her. . . .

"AHHHHH!" Laura screamed. She dived behind the goggles just in time. She peeked out to see an enormous dragonfly!

WHOMP! WHOMP! It hovered so close that she could hear its beating wings and feel the wind in her hair.

Wait. How is that dragonfly as big as I am? Laura thought.

"Oh no." She let out a groan.

"I've shrunk to the size of a bug!"

Suddenly, booming footsteps made the desk begin to shake.

"DOOOOCTOOOR BEEEEEE?" a thundering voice called.

Gabe, Olive, and Cesar entered the lab. Laura couldn't believe her eyes. They were *huge!*

"Gabe! Down here!" Laura cried, waving her arms wildly. But her friends couldn't hear her.

Dr. Bunsen emerged from the storage room. "Well, if it isn't the rest of the young DATA Set!" Dr. Bunsen was holding a new magnifying lens.

"Where's Laura? We thought she was here," Gabe said.

"I can see why she left." Cesar cringed at all the bugs in the room. "Uh, Dr. B., when was the last time you cleaned this place?"

Dr. Bunsen scratched his head.

"The cleaning service was just here."

A roach scurried up the wall next to Cesar. "Yeah, I'm gonna say they didn't do a good job."

"It looks like you've invited every bug in town here!" said Olive.

"I'll go get some bug spray," Dr. B. said. He placed the magnifying lens on the table.

Meanwhile, Laura still tried to get her friends' attention.

"DATA Set! HELLLLLP!!!" she yelled.

"Hey, did you hear something?" Gabe asked the others.

"You mean *other* than a million bugs buzzing and crawling around?" Cesar asked.

Laura huffed. She needed to find a way to get their attention. With a running leap, she jumped and pinched Gabe's hand.

"OW!" yelped Gabe. "I think a bug just bit me!"

As Laura toppled down, Olive caught a glimpse of her blue shirt.

"That's a weird-looking bug," Olive said. She picked up the magnifying lens Bunsen had left and peered through it.

"Holy caterpillar!" she cried. "It's Laura!"

The DATA Set crowded around the lens.

"What happened to you?" asked
Cesar. "Why are you so tiny?"

Laura urgently pointed over to
the shrink ray.

"Are you dancing?" Cesar asked.
"You danced yourself tiny? You're
a tiny dancer?"

Laura smacked her head. Then

as she ran toward the shrink ray, there was a familiar sound.

WHOMP. WHOMP.

This time there was nowhere to hide. The dragonfly snatched Laura and flew out the window!

"Laura!" her friends cried.

Chapter 4

To the Rescue

"We have to go after Laura!" exclaimed Gabe. "Before that bug eats her!"

"Maybe it won't," said Cesar. "Maybe it only eats leaves."

Gabe shook his head. "Dragonflies definitely eat other bugs. We need to get outside now."

When the three friends turned to leave, Cesar accidently bumped into the shrink ray.

The machine began to glow blue, then red, and then . . .

ZAP! ZAP! ZAP!

It shrunk all three kids!

"Um, what just happened?" Olive cried. She looked around the giant room.

"We're tiny like Laura!" said Gabe.

"Ohhhhhh, so *that's* what Laura meant. She didn't dance herself tiny. That invention turned her tiny," said Cesar. "Boy, I have really got to stop bumping into things."

"Dr. B. can help us," said Olive as the hulking doc- tor came back to the room.

"Dr. Bunsen!" the kids all yelled at the top of their lungs.

But the doctor couldn't hear them. Instead, he looked around the lab. "Now the *rest* of the DATA Set has run off too?" He shook his head. "These blasted bugs are driving everyone away!"

Bunsen narrowed his eyes as he sized up the bugs. "Well, my creepy-crawly friends, you may not be repelled by my Bug-Away-400, but *this* bug spray is one hundred percent guaranteed to keep you away! *Huzzah!*"

The doctor sprayed every corner of the lab.

"Oh no. Get out of the way!" Gabe cried as he covered his mouth. Bunsen had aimed right at them!

"Dr. B., stop!" cried Cesar.

"He can't hear you," Gabe said.

"Just like we couldn't hear Laura."

"Then what are we going to do?" asked Olive.

A determined look spread across Gabe's face. "We need to find Laura first. It's going to get dark soon."

"Uh . . ." Cesar looked uncertain. "Are you sure it's a good idea to go outside? You know—since we're all bug-size, we probably shouldn't

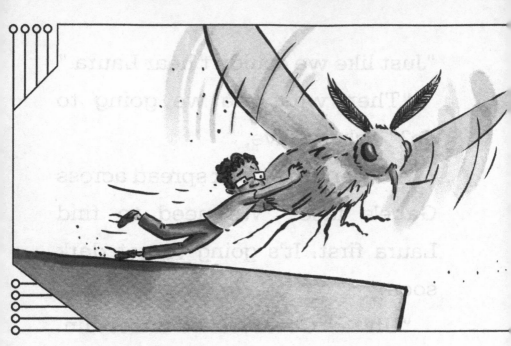

go looking for reasons to get eaten.
There must be another way."

Gabe shook his head. "Laura's
out there alone. She needs us!
Come on, guys. The DATA Set
always sticks together. Are you
with me?"

Cesar and Olive looked at each other and then nodded.

"Good, because our rides are leaving!" Gabe yelled. "Let's go!"

As three bugs flew past, the DATA Set hopped on and hoped for the best.

Chapter 5

Don't Look Down!

"Ahhhhhhhhh!" screamed Cesar. "I really don't think this was a good idea!"

The kids sailed out the window and high into the air. They each rode on their own bug.

"You'll be fine! Just don't look down!" called Gabe.

"How do we find Laura?" Olive shouted.

"With some DATA Set luck," said Gabe as he pointed ahead.

The dragonfly held on tight to

Laura as they hovered low to the ground.

"Laura!" the three friends cried as they flew to her side.

"DATA Set?!" she exclaimed. "What are you doing?"

"Rescuing you!" cried Gabe.

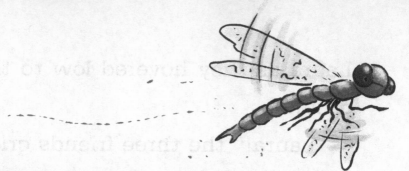

"But how did—ahhhhh!" Laura slipped and fell into the grass!

"Laura!" her friends screamed.

"We need to jump," exclaimed Gabe. "On the count of three!"

"You said don't look down!" groaned Cesar. "Now you want us to jump?"

"If we are as small as insects, then we'll be fine!" said Olive.

"If?" yelped Cesar.

Gabe nodded and hoped Olive was right. "Ready? One, two, three!"

They each let go of their bugs
and plummeted downward.

"I HATE THREE!!!!!" screamed
Cesar.

Pfff! Pfff! Pfff!

The kids landed safely on the ground.

"Is everyone okay?" Gabe asked.

"Yeah, I guess that wasn't so bad," replied Cesar.

"I told you." Olive helped him to his feet. "Since we are tiny, our mass and weight are different from before. Falling through air at this size is more like falling through water. Simple physics."

Cesar looked at Gabe. "Did you know that would happen?"

"I was pretty sure," said Gabe. "Now let's go find Laura!"

The friends trudged through the maze of tall grass blades that seemed like trees in a jungle.

"This is going to be impossible." Cesar whacked a stem out of his way. The stalk swung back at him, raining down white fluff.

"Achoo! Dandelions!" Cesar sneezed. "Can't . . . breathe . . ."

Gabe rolled his eyes. "Just brush it off and keep watch for Laura."

Cesar huffed. Gabe's words stung like a bee. "Fine—after all, we always do what you say."

"What's that supposed to mean?" said Gabe.

"You always do this," said Cesar. "You always insist we do whatever you say because you're the leader."

Now Gabe's feelings were hurt. "That's not true!"

"It is *so* true," argued Cesar. "We are in this buggy trouble because of you—"

"Guys, now isn't the best time to fight," said Olive as she looked around. "Hey! There's something over that hill!"

The friends clambered up and over a small dirt pile.

There was Laura!

Gabe and the others ran to her side. "Are you okay?"

"Shhhhhhhhh." Laura pointed toward a tall clump of grass.

Staring back at them was an enormous grasshopper.

And it looked hungry.

Chapter 6

A Buggy Plan

"Three words," whispered Cesar. "Bug. Sized. Trouble."

"It's okay," Gabe said hesitantly. "Grasshoppers only eat plants."

The giant beast leaned down toward Gabe and opened its jaws.

"Ahhhhh!" Gabe threw up his hands.

CHOMP.

The grasshopper took a big bite from a dandelion stalk.

Munch. Munch.

The DATA Set watched and held their breath as the grasshopper leaped out of sight.

Laura turned to her tiny friends.

"Wow, am I glad to see you all! How did you get shrunk down?"

"That was my bad," said Cesar. "I bumped into Dr. B.'s shrink ray."

"Oh, Cesar." Laura couldn't help giggling.

Olive smiled. "It all worked out, though, because we found you!"

"Thanks for coming after me

even though I ran away earlier,"
said Laura.

"About that . . . I'm sorry I
broke your magnifying lens," said
Cesar.

"Thanks, Cesar. I'm sorry too,"
said Laura. "I got upset because
you were all joking around while I
was working."

"We wanted to help you, but we aren't all great at fixing things," said Gabe. "That's what you bring to the DATA Set."

"Well, we definitely need to help each other now. What do we do next?" asked Olive.

"We get back to Dr. B.'s house," Gabe said. "And I think . . ."

Suddenly, Gabe paused.

"What?" pressed Olive.

"Well, everyone might not like *my* idea." Gabe glanced over at Cesar.

"Aw, come on!" Cesar groaned.

"What's going on?" Laura asked.

"Cesar's mad because Gabe's

always the one with the plan,"
Olive explained.

"No, it's because he always leads
us into trouble," Cesar said.

"You didn't have to come with
us—" said Gabe.

"Guys, come on!" Laura interrupted. "We can't keep fighting."

Then she told the others about Dr. B. and his old partner. "If we don't work together, then we could end up like them. I'm not going to give up on the DATA Set."

The others were silent.

Cesar spoke first. "Gabe, your plan did help us find Laura. I'm sorry for getting so upset."

"That's okay, Cesar," said Gabe. "I should have made sure everyone agreed with the plan. Sorry if I was pushy too."

Olive grinned. "So are we all one big, happy team again?"

Laura put her hand out. "I'm in."

Gabe, Olive, and Cesar nodded and put their hands out too.

"Looks like the DATA Set is back!" Laura cheered.

"So, team, how do we get back inside?" asked Gabe.

Cesar chuckled. "We could always ride another bug."

The friends looked at one another.

"Good thinking, Cesar! That does makes sense," Olive said slowly.

"Wait. No. I was just kidding," said Cesar nervously.

Gabe smiled. "Cesar's plan sounds perfect to me."

Cesar sighed as he looked at his friends' eager faces. "Okay, fine. I can't believe I'm going to say this, but let's round up that grasshopper and go for a ride."

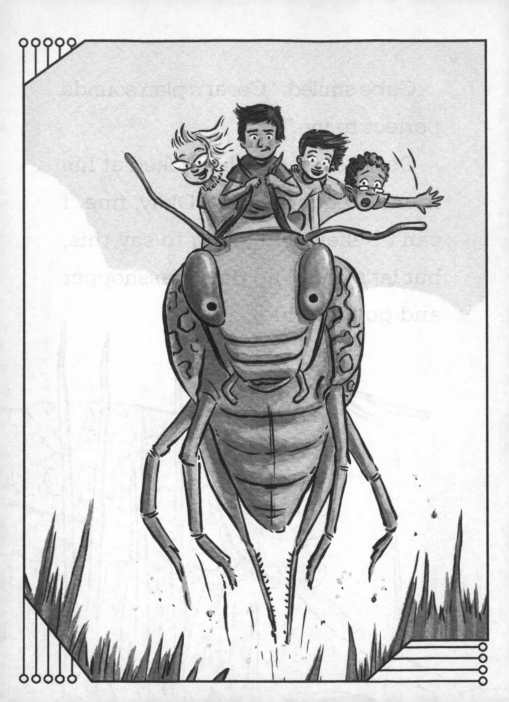

Chapter 7

Beetles and Termites and Bees, Oh My!

Cesar was back on a bug. And he was *not* happy about it.

"I've made up my mind!" he cried. "I. Hate. Bugs!!!"

The DATA Set rode a grasshopper across Dr. Bunsen's lawn. Gabe had distracted it with a piece of grass while the kids all climbed on board. Laura even made reins to hold on to out of grass.

"This is incredible!" Gabe was having the time of his life.

"And look! We're heading right to Dr. B.'s house!" Laura pointed.

The grasshopper bounded past

a large tomato plant in the vegetable garden. Gabe, Olive, and
Laura ducked, but Cesar smacked
into a leaf and fell to the ground.

"Cesar!" cried Olive.

"Quick!" yelled Laura. "Grab that
dandelion stalk!"

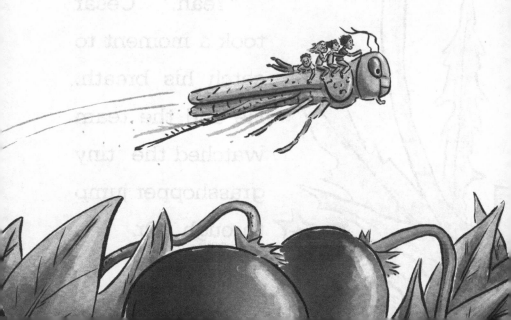

They grabbed hold of the stem and slid down as the grasshopper whizzed past.

Olive ran up to Cesar. "Are you okay?"

"Yeah." Cesar took a moment to catch his breath. He and the team watched the tiny grasshopper jump through Dr. B.'s open window. "Ugh, there goes our ride."

"It's okay," said Gabe. "We'll find a . . ." He looked around and his voice trailed off.

They were surrounded by *hundreds* of insects in the vegetable patch! Ants. Aphids. Beetles.

Termites and worms. Even bees and butterflies flitted overhead.

"Dr. B.'s bug problem is *bad*," said Cesar.

"I have never seen so many different types of bugs in one place!" exclaimed Gabe.

"They're all heading to the

window," exclaimed Laura. "Look!"

One by one, each and every bug crawled into Dr. Bunsen's lab.

"Hmm, Dr. B. was working on a bug-deterrent machine," Laura said slowly. "Do you think that it's doing the exact opposite and attracting bugs instead?"

"That's why there are so many bugs in Newtonburg!" exclaimed Olive.

"Dr. B. really *is* inviting them!" agreed Cesar.

"So all we need to do is get another ride back through the window," said Laura.

Gabe grinned. "Exactly! And these ants are our best bet. They

can carry up to five thousand times their own body weight. What do you say, DATA Set?"

Cesar nodded. "Fine. We can ride another bug. But only because I trust you . . . and because they don't fly."

Gabe smiled widely. "To the ants!"

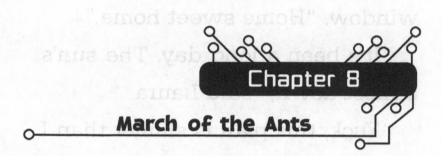

Chapter 8

March of the Ants

Four figures rose up and over the vast expanse of leaves winding around Dr. B.'s garden trellis. The setting sun beamed against their backs, casting tiny shadows.

The kids were riding ants like cowboys on horses, except their horses had six legs and climbed straight up the side of the house.

Gabe pointed to the open lab window. "Home sweet home."

"It's been a long day. The sun's almost down," said Laura.

"Yuck, this plan is slimier than I thought it would be." Cesar peeled his hand from the ant's gooey back.

"That's honeydew," explained Olive. "It's a sugary substance aphids make that ants eat. It looks like your ant is a messy eater."

"Ugh." Cesar stuck out his tongue in disgust. "I am not cut out to be a bug wrangler."

"Hold on, guys! We're almost there!" said Gabe.

The ants trudged along as the kids held on tightly.

"There's one problem," Laura said. "We need to get Dr. B.'s attention.

He can't hear us, remember?"

"I know," said Gabe. "We can

jump on him so he notices us."

"Notice us . . . or squash us like bugs," said Cesar.

Gabe nodded. "Well, I'm sure we'll come up with something."

The window ledge was very close now. Gabe's ant was leading the way until it stopped marching.

"Whoa!" exclaimed Gabe. "Why is my ant stopping?"

"Hey, mine is too." Olive nudged her ant, but it wouldn't move.

"Here's the problem," said Gabe. He reached down to pluck at the white strings that covered the ant path. The white material was sticky, and before Gabe could stop himself, he was tangled up in it!

"I've got a bad feeling about this!" Cesar exclaimed.

The friends looked down and gasped. Their ants had marched right into a spiderweb!

"Here, grab my hand!" Laura reached out to Gabe. But then her ant started wriggling against the sticky web, and she toppled forward.

"Yuck!" She splatted face-first into the web.

The vibrations knocked Olive off-balance too. "Whoa!" Now she was stuck on her back.

"Cesar, don't move!" warned Gabe. "You're the only one who's free!"

"Uh, the spiderweb isn't the bad news. That is!" Cesar stared beyond his friends, where an enormous spider was crawling toward its next meal.

Chapter 9

Spider Attack!

"This does not look good," said Cesar. "That spider set up shop here on purpose. It's been eating the bugs going through Dr. B.'s window. And we're next!"

"I can't move," Laura said.

"Me either," said Olive. "We're stuck."

"Stay calm, everybody. We need to put our heads together and figure a way out," declared Gabe.

The friends watched nervously as the spider crawled along the perimeter of the web.

"I think I've found my least favorite insect," said Cesar.

"Actually, a spider is not an insect," said Olive. "They are arachnids. They have two body sections instead of three, eight legs instead of six, and eight simple eyes instead of two compound eyes. Oh, and they don't have any antennae."

"Thanks for the lesson, but I'm more worried about saving you," said Cesar. "Any other fun spider facts that might get you unstuck?"

"That's it!" realized Olive. "Not all of the web strands are sticky. Spiders use the hairs on their legs to crawl along the nonsticky

ones. If you spot the strands without the glue dots on them, you can move anywhere on the web."

"But what if I break the web?" Cesar asked.

Gabe shook his head. "Spider silk is super strong. And even if

we do fall, remember, we're tiny!
We'll be all right."

"You can do it!" said Laura.

Cesar watched as the spider
moved closer and closer. He noticed
a small leaf stuck in the web.

Cesar gazed up at the other
leaves. They were holding the

entire web in place! "You said we'd be okay if we fell, right?"

"What are you going to do?" asked Gabe.

"I've got an idea! If I can't break the web, then I can channel my inner bug!" cried Cesar.

He took his first step onto a non-sticky thread. Then he quickly tip-toed across and reached the two main leaves that held the web. The spider spotted Cesar, but it was only a few inches from the other kids!

"Whatever you have in mind, do it now!" cried Olive.

With a huge *CHOMP*, Cesar started munching right through the leaves holding up the web, just like a bug would!

Gabe smiled. "Brace yourselves! Once those leaves are broken, this web will fall and release us to the ground."

As Cesar gnawed the leaves, the spider was closing in fast. The web wobbled as the creature was almost on top of him. And then . . .

Snap! Snap!

The leaves broke! Everything came tumbling down—kids, ants, and all!

FFFWOOOMP!

One by one, they each landed on a rose at the base of the trellis.

The ants and spider continued past them, tumbling safely to the ground.

"Wow, Cesar!" Olive jumped to hug him. "That was awesome!"

"Maybe I'm getting the hang of this bug thing after all." Cesar grinned.

"So what now?" asked Laura. "Should we try hitching one more ride up through the window?"

Gabe shrugged. "Maybe the third time's the charm? And it looks like we might just catch a lucky break."

He pointed to a group of bees

that were heading straight for the window.

"On three?" Gabe asked his friends.

They each nodded. "On three!"

Chapter 10

Dr. B.'s Busy Bees

"Confound it!" Dr. Bunsen dropped his tools to the floor. All around him were bugs, bugs, and more bugs!

"My invention is one hundred percent *buggy*." The doctor buried his face in his hands. "I suppose it's time to call Icky Lou's Pest Control."

As he reached for the phone, a loud buzzing filled his ears.

"Shoo, shoo." The doctor waved away four pesky bees. "I'm in no mood for this."

But the bees didn't go away. Instead, they kept flying around his head.

"Please, bees! Stop!" yelped the doctor.

Then he heard something very strange: a teeny-tiny voice. "Beeee!"

"Did this bee just . . . speak to me?" The doctor looked at the black and yellow insects hovering next to him. "Oh dear. I need to get out more."

"BEEEEEEEEEEEE!" the bees continued to whine.

"How odd," said the doctor. He slid down his magnifying goggles for a closer look.

The bees seemed much larger now. And there was someone riding each one!

"Newton's whiskers!" the doctor proclaimed. "DATA Set?!"

"DR. BEEEEEEEEEE!" they cried.

"How on earth did you all grow so tiny?" the doctor asked.

The friends landed next to his shrink ray.

"Ah, yes, I should have warned

you about that," said the doctor. "Quite a finicky invention. Goes off at the slightest touch. But never fear! I have just the thing to make you DATA Set size again!"

The doctor hurried into the storage room and returned.

He had the growth ray that had turned the toy animal figures to life!

"NOOO!" The friends all flailed their arms.

"It's quite all right." The doctor carefully clicked the settings on the device. "It's strictly a growth ray now."

The friends closed their eyes.

Dr. Bunsen focused the growth ray and smiled. "Everyone say 'fleas'! One, two, *huzzah!*"

In a bright flash he zapped Gabe, Laura, Cesar, and Olive. In an instant, the kids were back to ordinary size!

"*Huzzah!*" cheered the friends, hugging one another.

"*Huzzah* indeed!" said the doctor.

"But where have you been all this time?"

"We were bzzz-y solving the invasion of the insects, Dr. B.," said Laura. "Your Bug-Away-400 has been attracting all the bugs in Newtonburg, maybe even the world, to your house!"

The doctor's machine was now completely covered with creepy-crawly critters. "Do you think so?"

"We're pretty sure you have created the first Bug-on-Over-to-My-House-400," said Gabe.

"I suppose I could try reversing the signal," said the doctor. He flipped a tiny switch at the top of the machine.

The humming of the Bug-Away-400 was replaced by a high-pitched whine. All the bugs in the room scattered away and left Newtonburg.

Dr. Bunsen did a little jig as the kids laughed. "Well, now we are one hundred percent *bug free!*"